Disney

PIRATES of the CARIBBEAN
AT WORLD'S END

The Journey to World's End

Adapted by Tisha Hamilton

Based on characters created by Ted Elliott & Terry Rossio
and Stuart Beattie and Jay Wolpert
Written by Ted Elliott & Terry Rossio
Based on Walt Disney's Pirates of the Caribbean
Produced by Jerry Bruckheimer
Directed by Gore Verbinski

Part Two

Reader's Digest Children's Books

Pleasantville, New York • Montréal, Québec • Bath, United Kingdom

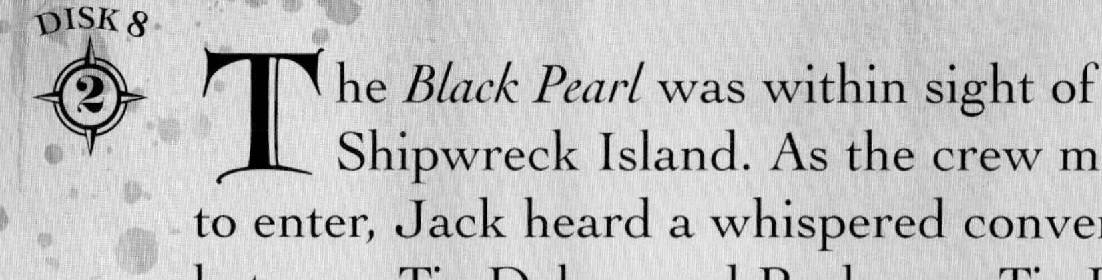

The *Black Pearl* was within sight of Shipwreck Island. As the crew made ready to enter, Jack heard a whispered conversation between Tia Dalma and Barbossa. Tia Dalma grabbed Barbossa's arm and watched as it decayed into a skeleton arm. "Do not forget it was my power that brought you back from the dead," she reminded him.

Now Jack knew why Barbossa was helping Tia Dalma. She had saved him—which also explained why he was now helping Jack, even though Jack had been the one to kill him on *Isla de Muerta*. Tia Dalma had ordered Barbossa to help.

With Jack at the wheel, the *Black Pearl* and its crew headed straight for the looming cliffs of Shipwreck Island. Hidden among the rocks was a narrow sea tunnel that led to a round cove in the center of the island. This was Shipwreck Cove and its city was made from the wrecks of broken ships. Pirate ships of all kinds filled the cove. The *Black Pearl* prepared to join them.

"There's not been a gathering like this in our lifetime," Barbossa remarked.

"And I owe all of them money," Jack added.

Meanwhile, aboard the *Flying Dutchman* was Will Turner. Jones had found him floating in the sea. Now Turner was at the mercy of the *Dutchman's* captain—and Beckett. The *Endeavour* had caught up!

It appeared the East India Trading Company's forces were gathering. Now they just had to find the pirates' hideout.

Since Jack had left him behind, Will couldn't tell Beckett how to find Shipwreck Cove. Jones was ready to kill him, but Beckett had a better idea. Beckett had taken Jack's Compass from Will when he'd captured him. Beckett knew it always pointed to whatever the person holding it wanted the most. He told Will about Elizabeth, who was surely in Shipwreck Cove as the captain of the *Empress*. He handed him the Compass.

"What is it you want the most?" Beckett asked.

DISK 9

1

The needle swung wildly and then settled. They had their heading.

In Shipwreck Cove, the Brethren Court was called to order. Eight swords stabbed into a nearby globe showed that eight of the nine Lords were present. "Your Pieces of Eight, my fellow captains," Barbossa rasped, nodding down at a wooden bowl on the table filled up with an assortment of strange objects. They were short two tokens.

"Sparrow," hissed the terse Pirate Lord Villanueva.

Jack smiled and toyed with his Piece of Eight. He, too, was waiting for the ninth Pirate Lord. Until the last Lord arrived, he would hold onto his token.

Suddenly, Elizabeth Swann entered the room. When she stabbed her sword into the globe, there was a rumbling among the Pirate Lords. She was a Pirate Lord, too.

"Listen to me," she told them urgently. "Our location is betrayed! Jones and the *Flying Dutchman* are under the command of Lord Beckett, and they are on their way here! We must prepare to fight them."

Mistress Ching, ancient and hardened, yet a Pirate Lord nonetheless, spoke up. "There is no need to fight. Shipwreck Cove is a fortress. They cannot get to us here."

Barbossa saw his chance. "There is a third course," he began.

"In another age, on this very spot, the first Brethren Court captured the Sea Goddess, and bound her in her bones. That was a mistake. We tamed the sea for ourselves, aye, but we also tamed it for the likes of Beckett and his ilk. It was better when mastery of the sea came by the sweat of a man's brow and the strength of his back—and not from bargains made with eldritch creatures like the Sea Goddess."

The other Pirate Lords began to nod among themselves. They knew what Barbossa said was true. He pressed his advantage, "We must free Calypso!" At this, the room erupted into argument.

The serene and priestly-looking Pirate Lord, Sri Sumbhajee, never spoke aloud. He simply motioned with his hands and his bodyguards interpreted his gestures. Now he flicked his wrist. "Sri Sumbhajee says," his guard translated, "Barbossa has lost his senses! Do not let him speak any further!" Many of the other Pirate Lords agreed, with cries of "Shoot him!" and "Cut out his tongue!"

Another Pirate Lord, Gentleman Jocard summed up their opinion when he said, "Calypso was our enemy then! She will be our enemy now!"

Yet others, like Elizabeth, spoke up on behalf of Barbossa's plan. She thought Calypso could help. But she also believed they would still need to fight—Calypso or no Calypso. Soon guns and swords were drawn and fists were flying. These were pirates, after all. They very rarely agreed.

Back in the brig of the *Black Pearl,* Tia Dalma calmly scattered her crab claws and read the patterns that they made. She knew what was coming next. She always did. Tia Dalma stood and turned to face Davy Jones, who was standing in the shadows with his pistol pointed right at her.

Tia Dalma gasped at the monster Davy Jones had become. She knew he had once been a man. She touched the place where his heart once beat and he began to transform. Gone was the tentacled half-man, half-beast he had become. He was young and handsome—and human—once again.

Then she pulled her hand away and Jones turned back into the monster he'd become.

Back inside Shipwreck Cove, Barbossa banged a cannonball on the table while pirates brawled all around him. Finally, the pirates began to settle down. "It was the first court that imprisoned Calypso," he tried to persuade them. "None of us were among that group. If we set her free now, surely she will reward us."

"Or at least she will reward the one who summoned us to do so," Jack pointed out shrewdly. He didn't trust Barbossa. "I agree with Captain Swann. We must fight."

As the Pirate Lords began their debate again, Barbossa thought of one more ploy. "If we fight, it be an act of war," he insisted. "And war can only be declared by the Pirate King."

A Pirate King had to be elected by the Pirate Lords, yet they were all so selfish each would only vote for himself.

"I call for a vote," Jack called out. One by one, each of the Pirate Lords cast a vote.

"I vote for Ammand the Corsair," cried Ammand.

"Capitaine Chevalle, the penniless Frenchman!" chimed Chevalle.

DISK 10

1

"Mistress Ching!" And so it went. Each Lord voting for themself. It looked as if there would again be no Pirate King elected.

But then Jack voted. The room erupted. The Pirate King had been chosen. The Pirate Lords were going to war!

The Pirate Lords assembled their armada: the *Black Pearl*, the *Empress*, and many other ships. Together, they sailed out into the mist surrounding Shipwreck Island. As the *Endeavour* emerged from the fog, the pirates let out a bloodcurdling roar. This fancy armored ship was no match for the Pirate Lords. This war would be over before it began.

Then the fog began to clear and the pirates saw not one ship, but hundreds and hundreds. All heavily armed, all pointing straight at Shipwreck Island. The chilling sight of the *Flying Dutchman* rising up from beneath the waves to lead them silenced the pirates once and for all. Angry pirate eyes turned to Jack Sparrow, the man who'd led them into this.

"Parley?" Jack suggested. Perhaps a meeting could avert a disastrous battle.

The parley was arranged, and two longboats pulled onto a strip of beach. Beckett, Davy Jones, and Will Turner climbed onto the sand from one boat. Jack, Barbossa, and Elizabeth were in the other.

Barbossa accused Will of treachery. Beckett accused Jack of masterminding the doublecross. Jones cut through the conversations. "Your debt to me must still be paid," he insisted to Jack.

Elizabeth glanced at Will. He gave a nearly invisible nod. "I propose an exchange," she ventured. "Will leaves with us, and you can have Jack."

The deal was almost done when Barbossa began to suspect a rat. He grabbed hold of Jack, sending his Piece of Eight spinning to the ground where it was promptly picked up by "Jack" the monkey. Jack couldn't get it back now. He was leaving with Beckett and Jones.

Before he walked away, Beckett gave the pirates one last bit of advice, "Tell your Brethren this: you can fight, and all of you will die. Or you can not fight, in which case only most of you will die."

Barbossa, Elizabeth, and Will climbed back aboard the *Black Pearl*.

"Barbossa, you can't release her," Will warned, knowing that Barbossa planned on setting Calypso free.

Barbossa smiled and wrapped his fist around Elizabeth's Piece of Eight. Then he yanked it from her.

"I can now," Barbossa told him. He had all nine of the Pirate Lords' tokens. As he placed them in the bowl, the wind died. The tokens began to smolder and, as the words were spoken, burst into flame.

"Calypso, I release you from your human bonds!"

The final battle had now been set in motion. Elizabeth knew the pirates needed to work together or all would be lost. After all, Calypso might not help the Lords now that she was freed. Elizabeth was determined not to give up without a fight. She made an impassioned speech. "Listen to me! Are we frightened bilge rats? No! We are free! Let's show our enemy the flash of our cannons! Let them hear the ring of our swords! Then we will show what we can do by the sweat of our brows and the strength of our backs."

At this, she nodded to Barbossa, who remembered his own words. "And the courage of our hearts," she finished.

"Hoist the colors!" rang the cry from every pirate's lips. "Hoist the colors!"

The seas were about to grow very stormy.

And *both* sides were prepared to weather the tempest and emerge victorious.

-The End-